JENNY

BY

BETH P. WILSON

ILLUSTRATED BY

DOLORES JOHNSON

Macmillan Publishing Company   New York

To a Jenny I know
and all the special
Jennys in the world
— B. P. W.

In memory of my mother,
who encouraged me in so many ways
— D. J.

Text copyright © 1990 by Beth P. Wilson • Illustrations copyright © 1990 by Dolores Johnson • All rights reserved. No part of this book may be reproduced or transmitted in any form or by any means, electronic or mechanical, including photocopying, recording, or by any information storage and retrieval system, without permission in writing from the Publisher. Macmillan Publishing Company, 866 Third Avenue, New York, NY 10022. Collier Macmillan Canada, Inc.

Printed and bound in Singapore   First American Edition   10 9 8 7 6 5 4 3 2 1

The text of this book is set in 14 point Aldus. The illustrations are rendered in watercolor on paper.

Library of Congress-in-Publication Data

Wilson, Beth P. Jenny / by Beth P. Wilson; illustrated by Dolores Johnson. — 1st American ed.   p.   cm. Summary: In a series of brief monologues, Jenny shares her delight in the things that fill her world, from family and school to bubble baths, a wedding, chocolate cookies, and the memory of Martin Luther King.

ISBN 0-02-793120-X

[1. Afro-Americans — Fiction.] I. Johnson, Dolores, ill. II. Title.   PZ7.W6898Je 1990   [E] — dc20   89-8135   CIP   AC

JENNY

I am Jenny
and I love everybody
in the whole world.

SOMETIMES I WONDER

Sometimes I wonder about the sky
up there so high, an' the earth
down below, about trees growin'
so tall without topplin' over,
an' oceans pushin' jump waves
back an' forth.
I wonder about the moon, too, an'
birds flyin'.
God must have put everything in
place an' said, *"GO!"*

WISHING

I wish I lived way out
on a little farm. Then
I could feed the chickens
'n' everything and have
lots of fun and breathe
the fresh air. Maybe I
could ride a pony, too.

An' maybe I'm jus' wishing.

THE STRONG WIND

When I walk along
the strong wind blowing
in my face feels cool-fresh,
cool-fresh.
Sometimes I throw my head
back and skip.
Then the wind tries to whirl
me about like an inside-out
umbrella.

I LIKE DR. KING

I like Dr. King because
he wanted everybody to
be happy. He was against
people fighting an' hating
each other.
I hate fighting, too.

JUDITH

Judith sits at her desk
looking straight ahead
like a sphinx.
She doesn't act like she's
alive except when someone
calls "Judith."
She used to be Judy
but now she's Judith—
and she likes that.

CRYING

Little Stevie is so funny.
He was talkin' 'bout people
cryin' an' he said, "When
people cry it's like when it
rains, excep' when you cry you
only get two drops." Pretty
smart, huh?
Excep' when I cry plenty drops
come runnin' down my face.

MY DADDY

My daddy came
to my birthday party.
He brought me a gold
necklace, a book, an'
a real pretty suit —
it's denim.
We had lots of fun!
Then after the party
he went back to his home
in Ohio.

SUNDAY BURGERS

Sometimes I go to Grandma's on weekends, but on Sunday after church, she's always cookin' a big dinner. That's when I wish I was at my own house 'cause me an' my mother would jus' get a good hamburger an' milk shake an' go to different places an' have lots of fun.

GRANDMA'S BABY PICTURES

When I go visiting with Grandma
she likes to show people my
baby pictures on her bracelet.
Her friends say, "I remember
when you were a baby." I don't
like that. It makes me feel shy.

MY TEACHER

Sometimes my teacher
sits quiet like a picture.
I think she must be wonderin'
about us.
When she smiles she seems
like a real person.
But when somethin' is funny
an' we all laugh together,
that's when I like her
best of all.

FLOWERS TO SCHOOL

Sometimes when I take flowers
to school, the stems get warm
in my hand. My teacher lets me
put them in a bowl of water,
just the way I please.
Then they look pretty
and I feel kinda special.

A SISTER OR BROTHER

I wish my mother would
get married again so
I could have a little
sister or brother. We've
been alone a long time —
every year we're alone.

THE BIG RAIN

My little cousin, Alexis,
was talkin' 'bout the big
rain las' night. She said,
"Didn't it rain hard? Ooh,
it rained an' rained! I think
God was takin' a big shower
an' his angels, too, only
they had to take off their
wings first."
Her mommy an' daddy laughed.
Then we all gave her a hug an'
kiss. She's so cute.

RUTHIE

Ruthie won't talk to me
because she has a new friend.
But don't you worry —
I'm goin' to win Ruthie
an' her friend in the end.

WHEN WE GROW UP

I asked Jinny what Sandy
and her was talking about when
they was sitting on that
bench an' sometimes they
giggled.
She said,
"Oh, we was just talking
about our mothers an' how
they treat us an' how we're
going to treat our children
when we grow up."

A FRIEND

I think those kids
was real mean to poke
fun at that new girl
jus' 'cause she's small
an' wears those big
thick eyeglasses. I
felt sorry for her
when she started to cry.
I went over an' put
my arm around her an'
I said, "I'll be your
friend." We walked all
around the playground.
Then she stopped cryin'.

THE ARCHED GATE

I saw a pretty gate
with a curve over the top.
It was painted white an'
had lovely colored flowers
around it.
When I grow up an' get
married, I'd like to have
one of those gates in my
front yard. Then the house would
look pretty like a bride's.

THE WEDDING

We went to a wedding yesterday.
The bride wore a long white dress
and she carried some lovely flowers.
She was so-o pretty. And the
little flower girl was pretty, too.
But the best part was when the
groom kissed the bride!
An' then the cake an' punch at the
reception — mmm.

BIG TREES

I like big trees.
Once, when it was
raining hard, I ran
an' stood under a
big tree with floppy
branches. It was my
friend because it covered
me like a giant umbrella.

GOIN' FISHIN'

Grandpa said if I wore
my jeans an' a boy's cap,
he'd take me fishing. We'd
have to get up early
in the morning, when it's
dark. An' I'd have to
sit still an' be quiet so
the fish would bite.
Grandpa said you have to go
fishin' to find out where
your head is.
After sittin' quiet so long
I had to find out
where my mouth was.

THREE-RING CIRCUS

When Grandpa took me to
the circus, I tried to see
everything at once. My head
was whirlin' round and round.
Then somebody bumped me an'
my big pail of popcorn went
flyin' all over the place.
Grandpa said, "Don't
worry, jus' watch the acrobats.
I'll buy you some cola and
another pail of popcorn."
We sure had a good time!

SUMMER GRASS

When I lie on the grass
the sun warms my body, blinks
my eyes, and makes me feel limp
and happy all over, right down
to the tips of my wiggly brown
toes.

BEACH WATER

Beach water is fun
to stomp around in,
but when I stoop to lift
the water in my arms
it feels heavy and
slips away to be with
the deep water again.

Good-bye, beach water.

I FOOLED MY MOTHER

You know me an' my mother
have fun. Saturday she wanted
me to help change her bed an'
I didn't want to. So she said,
"Come on, Jenny, we'll have
this bed made in no time."
I said, "Okay, the time's up
if it's no time." She laughed
but I really fooled her that
day.

THE BUBBLE BATH

I love a bubble bath.
When the tub is full
of bubbles, I'm a
princess in a castle.
I have a round bar of soap
that smells like rose petals.
It slips over my nice clean body.

Soon someone comes
with a soft bath towel
to dry me.

Soon the bubbles are gone
an' I'm just me again.

AT GRANDMA'S HOUSE

I'm goin' to my grandma's
tomorrow. I can hardly wait
'cause my grandma's lots
of fun. Sometimes we play
checkers. An' sometimes we dance.

I like to sleep at my
grandma's house. Grandmas
take good care of you. An'
they live a long time.

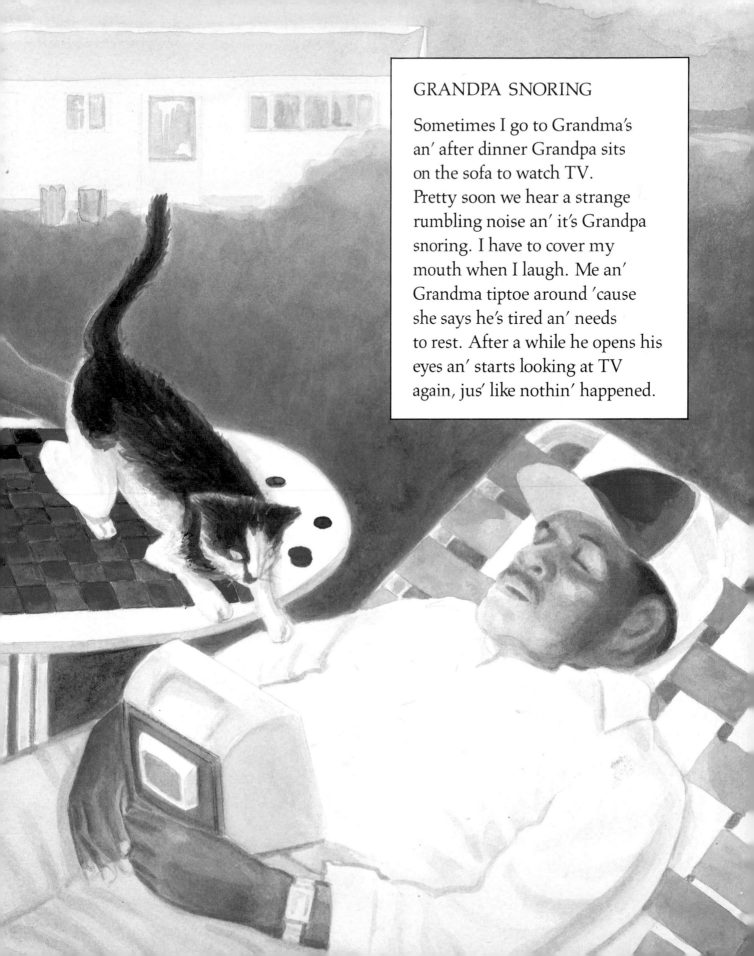

GRANDPA SNORING

Sometimes I go to Grandma's an' after dinner Grandpa sits on the sofa to watch TV. Pretty soon we hear a strange rumbling noise an' it's Grandpa snoring. I have to cover my mouth when I laugh. Me an' Grandma tiptoe around 'cause she says he's tired an' needs to rest. After a while he opens his eyes an' starts looking at TV again, jus' like nothin' happened.

CHOCOLATE COOKIES

Sandy's coming over to
my house an' we're going
to make chocolate cookies.
I can hardly wait because
the batter's so yum-yum
good. We lick it from the
spoon an' the 'lectric beaters.
It's better than anything
until the cookies are baked.

SPOOKY

You know what's spooky?
When somebody puts
something in paper
an' wraps it up tight,
an' pretty soon there's
a little cracky noise
an' the paper moves
an' starts to come
unwrapped.
The little cracky noise
comes again an' the paper
moves.
Ooh, that's *spooky*.

STERLING SILVER

When I eat dinner at Grandma's
I tell her I want to eat my
ice cream with her mother's
spoon. It's shiny an' thin an'
pretty. An' it tastes cold in my mouth.
Grandma says it's sterling silver.

CHRISTMAS IS COMING

When Christmas is coming
I help decorate the tree
an' my stocking gets filled
with goodies. My mother says
people are happy because they
are celebrating the birthday
of the baby Jesus. But Gail's family
doesn't celebrate Christmas
because they are Jehovah's
Witnesses, an' David doesn't
either because his family is
Jewish an' they celebrate
Hanukkah. An' Kirika doesn't
either because his family celebrates
an African festival. My mother
says it doesn't matter jus' so
you find a time to be thankful
an' happy.

I'M GOIN' TO PRAY FOR PEACE

I don't like war.
I saw some pictures on TV.
An' it was terrible!
When I say my prayers
I'm goin' to pray for peace.